This book
belongs to

CLIFFORD®
SCHOOL DAYS
TREASURY

By Norman Bridwell

Cartwheel ·B·O·O·K·S·®

SCHOLASTIC INC.

New York   Toronto   London   Auckland   Sydney
Mexico City   New Delhi   Hong Kong   Buenos Aires

Clifford's ABC
Copyright © 1983 by Norman Bridwell.

Count on Clifford
Copyright © 1985 by Norman Bridwell.

Clifford's Word Book
Copyright © 1990 by Norman Bridwell.

All rights reserved. Published by Scholastic Inc. CLIFFORD is a registered trademark of Norman Bridwell.
SCHOLASTIC, CARTWHEEL BOOKS, and associated logos are trademarks and/or registered trademarks of Scholastic Inc.

ISBN-13: 978-0-439-91568-7
ISBN-10: 0-439-91568-6

12 11 10 9 8 7 6 5 4 3 2 1   7 8 9 10 11 12/0

Printed in China   62

This collection first published, June 2007

Book design by Mark Freiman

Table of Contents

CLIFFORD®
ABC

Aa

Aa
accordion
acorns
alligator
anchor
ant
anvil
armadillo
axe

axe

accordion

armadillo

anvil

acorns

ant

anchor

alligator

Bb

bird

ball

bat

basket

balloon

boots

boy

boat

butterfly

beaver

bottle

baby

Bb
baby
ball
balloon
basket
bat
beaver
bird
boat
boots
bottle
boy
butterfly

Cc

Cc
cactus
cake
candle
cape
cat
checks
clown
collar
cook
cow

collar

cow

cat

cook

candle

cake

cactus

cape

clown

checks

Dd

dragon

dolphin

dog

dummy

derby

drum

dandelion

15

Ee
eagle

egg

Ee

eagle
earring
eel
egg
elephant
elf
Eskimo

earring

elephant

eel

elf

Eskimo

16

Ff

flag

frog

fly

fish

fire

fairy

flea

funnel

flower

fox

Gg

ghost

giraffe

gorilla

garden

goat

glove

garbage can

Gg
garbage can
garden
ghost
giraffe
glove
goat
gorilla

Hh

helicopter

harp

house

horse

hollyhock

hummingbird

hat

horn

haystack

hippopotamus

19

Ii

iguana

igloo

iris

ink

iron

ice cream cone

Ii
ice cream cone
igloo
iguana
ink
iris
iron

20

Jj

jet

juggler

jogger

jack-o'-lantern

jester

jacks

Jj
jack-o'-lantern
jacks
jester
jet
jogger
juggler

Kk   Ll

Kk
kangaroo
karate
kayak
kitten
knight
knitting
koala

Ll
lamb
lasso
leopard
lily
lion
lobster
log
lumberjack

koala

lobster

lily

lasso

knight

karate

knitting

kitten

lumberjack

log

kangaroo

kayak

leopard

lamb

lion

22

Mm

moon

mop

map

monkey

mask

mittens

mouse

marionette

magician

magnet

23

Nn

note

nest

nun

nutcracker

nut

net

nurse

noodles

Oo

owl

orchid

ostrich

orange

overalls

octopus

oar

parachute

palm

pineapple

P p

picture

panda

pirate

paintbrush

pear

palette

Pp
paintbrush
palette
palm
panda
parachute
pear
picture
pig
pineapple
pirate
pony
porcupine

pony

pig

porcupine

26

Qq

quail

quartet

quilt

question

queen

27

Rr
rabbit
raccoon
racket
radishes
rain
rainbow
rake
rhinoceros
robot
rocket
roller skate
rope
rug

rain

Rr

rainbow

rhinoceros

rocket

robot

rope

racket

rug

raccoon

rabbit

rake

roller skate

radishes

Ss

Saturn

star

scarecrow

sleep

soccer ball

saxophone

sausage

seesaw

sandwich

squirrel

snail

seal

stool

Ss
sandwich
Saturn
sausage
saxophone
scarecrow
seal
seesaw
sleep
snail
soccer ball
squirrel
star
stool

29

Tt
table
teapot
teddy bear
telescope
television
tent
tepee
tiger
tractor
train
turtle

tepee

tent

tractor

tiger

telescope

television

teapot

train

teddy bear

turtle

table

Uu

umbrella

UFO

unicorn

umpire

urn

ukulele

unicycle

Uu
UFO
ukulele
umbrella
umpire
unicorn
unicycle
urn

Vv

Vv
vacuum cleaner
valentine
vampire
vase
violets
violin
vise
volcano

volcano

vampire

valentine

violets

violin

vise

vacuum cleaner

vase

Ww

whale

waves

walrus

wrenches

wheelbarrow

witch

wolf

worm

waffles

wagon

W

Xx Yy

xylophone

yacht

x-ray

yak

Xx
x-ray
xylophone

Yy
yacht
yak
yarn
yawn
yo-yo

yawn

yarn

yo-yo

zeppelin

Zz

zebra

zipper

zither

ZOO

Zz
zebra
zeppelin
zipper
zither
zoo

z

35

For Timothy, Brian, and Julie Stanton

COUNT ON CLIFFORD®

38

Count **one** Clifford.

one

Hi! My name is Emily Elizabeth.

This is my dog, Clifford. There is only **one** Clifford in all the world.

HAPPY BIRTHDAY,
CLIFFORD

On Clifford's birthday, I gave him a party.

one

Count **one** Clifford.

two

We were going to have a lot of balloons.
I blew up **two** balloons. Then I got tired.

Clifford tried to blow up the rest. Clifford blew a little too hard, so we just had **two** balloons.

Count
two balloons.
Count **two** girls.
Count **two** boys.

two

three

Count **three** presents.

I bought Clifford **three** presents.
I wrapped them up. I was going
to put bows on them.

But Clifford found the ribbons first.
What a mess!

Count **three** windows.

three

four

Count
four party hats.

46

I invited Clifford's dog friends.
Four of them came.
I didn't ask any cats.

Count **four** of Clifford's dog friends.

Count **four** houses.

four

five

Count **five** chairs.
Count **two**
yellow chairs.

We played musical chairs.
I set up **five** chairs.

We ran around and around.
When the music stopped,
Clifford was the first
to sit down. No more
musical chairs.

five

six

Count **six** trees.

We played Hide-and-Seek. Clifford hid behind **six** trees.

We found Clifford anyway.

six

seven

Count
seven candles.

Count
seven forks.

Then it was time for Clifford's cake. I put **seven** candles on the cake.

Clifford blew out the candles.
We had ice cream instead.

seven

8

eight

Clifford opened his gifts.
Everyone had the same idea.

Clifford got **eight** sacks of dog food.

Count
four red sacks.

Count **four**
yellow sacks.

Count all
eight sacks.

eight

Count
four red balls.
Count **five**
yellow balls.
Count all
nine balls.

nine

We had a clown at the party.
The clown juggled **nine** balls.

Clifford wanted to juggle, too.
Oops!

9

nine

ten

Count **three** gray cats.
Count **three** white cats.
Count **four** striped cats.
Count all **ten** cats.

Then some cats came. They wanted to play games, too. We asked them to join us. They did. **One, two, three, four, five, six, seven, eight, nine, ten.**

Ten cats in all!

ten

We were having fun.
Then I felt a raindrop.

Count the children.

Count the dogs.

Don't forget to count Clifford.

Oh, no! It was raining.
The party would be ruined.

Count the boys.
Count the girls.

But Clifford knew what to do. He saved the party. I always knew I could count on Clifford.

Count the cats.
Count the dogs.
Count the party hats.

HAPPY BIRTHDAY, CLIFFORD!

dog house

CLIFFORD

Dedicated to Nadia Miret

CLIFFORD®
WORD BOOK

sky

house

tree

dog

grass

girl

My name is Emily Elizabeth
and this is my big red dog, Clifford.

picture

plant

clock

hook

Clifford is too big to fit inside my room.
But he can still keep me company.

bed

book

dresser

pillow

blanket

slippers

hanger

rug

radio

curtain

mirror

lamp
shade

light
switch

amp

brush

glass

windowsill

night
table

teddy bear

drawer

socks

mitt

baseball

Like all dogs, Clifford has a favorite toy. What's your favorite toy?

kite

football

glider

yo-yo

jump rope

rocking horse

wagon

train

toy car

70

soccer ball

bat

stuffed monkey

dinosaur

crayons

puzzle

tennis racket

tea set

dollhouse

carriage

baseball

blocks

top

rattle

jacks

doll

flag

streetlight

BARBER SHOP

barber pole

49

bananas

watermelons

pineapples

bench

fire hydrant

And he likes to go for walks.
This is the main street of our town.

Everybody knows Clifford.
And everybody likes Clifford.

police officer

nurse

doctor

letter carrier

astronaut

veterinarian

waiter

photographer	magician	baseball player	carpenter

chef	**farmer**	**jester**	**fire fighter**

auto mechanic	**musician**	**jockey**	**fisherman**

hat

chalkboard

$3 \times 3 = 9$

map

$$\begin{array}{r} 2 \\ +4 \\ \hline 6 \end{array}$$

clock

bookcase

pen

chalkboard eraser

chalk

globe

scissors

wastebasket

book

desk

boots

jacket

Clifford waits for me while I'm in school.
I can see him outside the window.

bulletin
board

poster

aquarium

crossing
guard

calendar

lunch box

scarf

chair

ruler

train

truck

unicycle

tugboat

jet

car

jeep

78

helicopter

hot-air balloon

race car

sailboat

Clifford likes things that move.
I tell him not to chase cars.
But sometimes he forgets.

motorcycle

canoe

basketball hoop

basketball

ice-cream vendor

birdbath

jogger

skateboard

pogo stick

In the afternoon, we play in the park.
Clifford is even more fun than a swing!

swings

jungle gym

fountain

picnic table

slide

sandbox

seesaw

guitar

trumpet

xylophone

tambourine

bow

violin

triangle

piano

saxophone

Clifford loves listening to music.
He is a good singer.

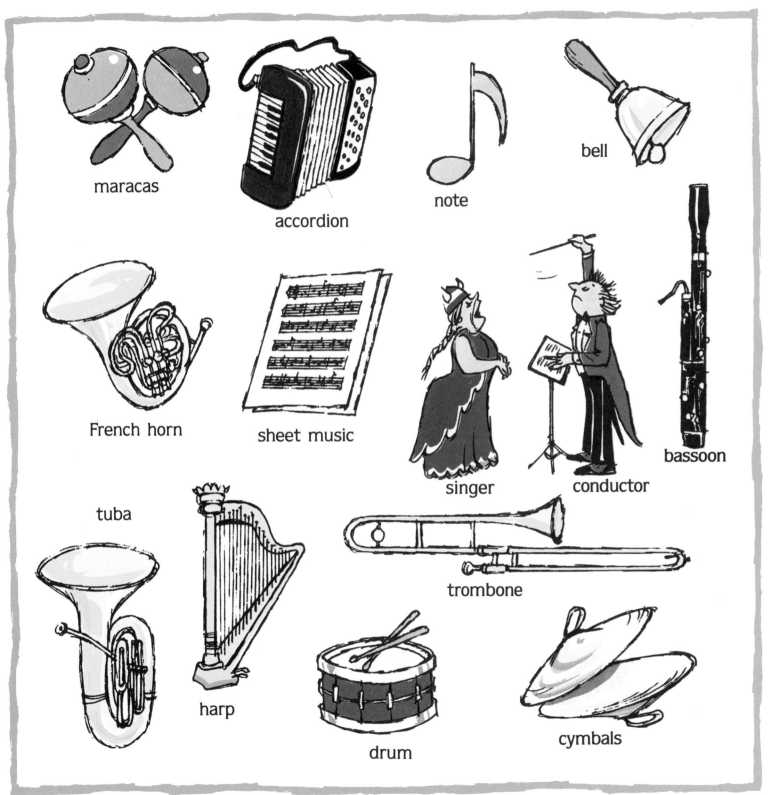

maracas

accordion

note

bell

French horn

sheet music

singer

conductor

bassoon

tuba

harp

trombone

drum

cymbals

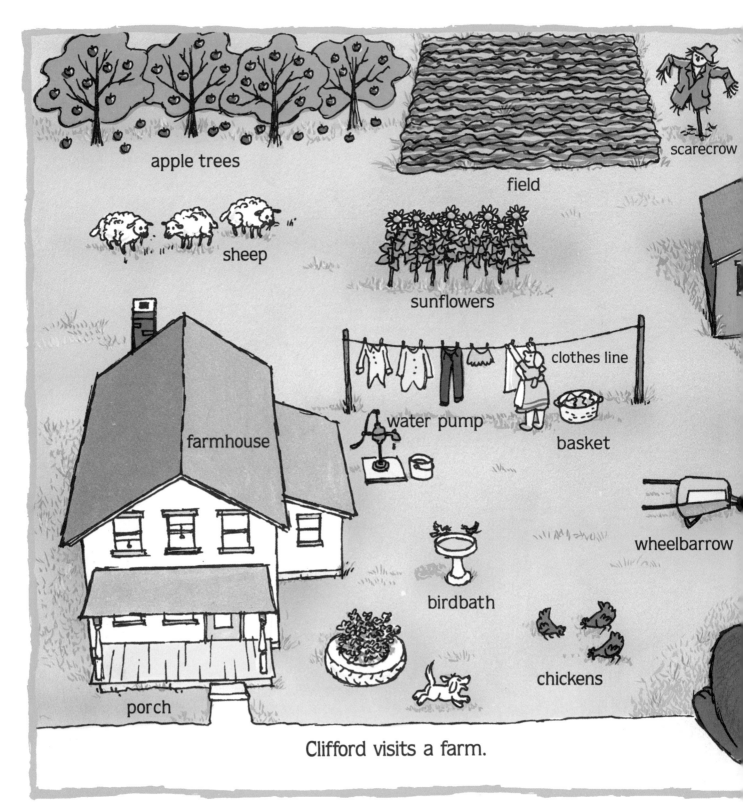

apple trees

field

scarecrow

sheep

sunflowers

clothes line

water pump

basket

farmhouse

birdbath

wheelbarrow

porch

chickens

Clifford visits a farm.

silo

pitchfork

haystack

cows

barn

rooster

horse

stable

tractor

pigs

fence

trapeze

Once the circus came to town.
Clifford helped to put on a show.

pie

hoop

ringmaster

tiger

juggler

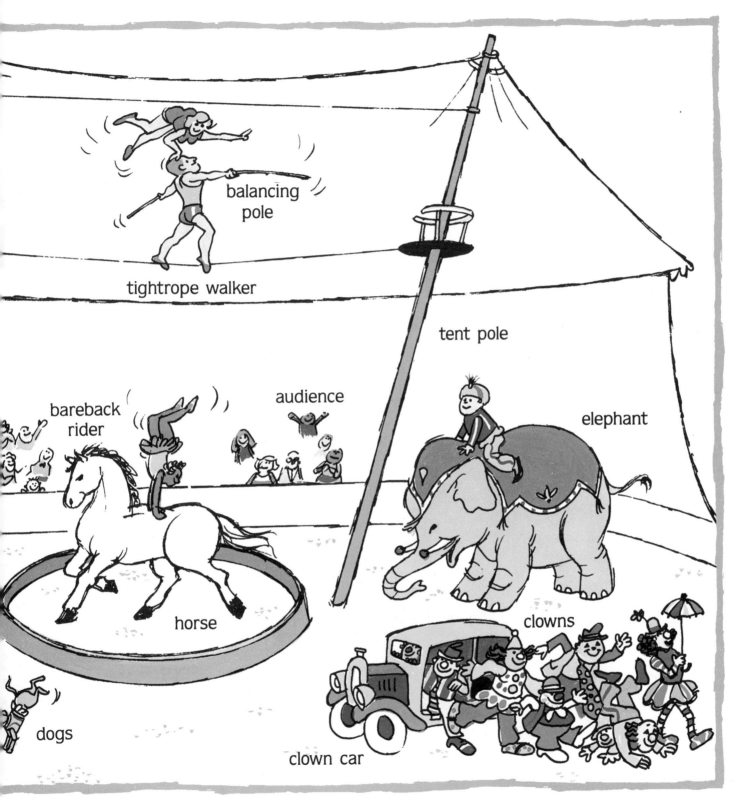

balancing pole

tightrope walker

tent pole

bareback rider

audience

elephant

horse

clowns

dogs

clown car

87

sea lion

turtle

camel

kangaroo

Clifford is bigger
than an elephant!

rhinoceros

penguin

octopus

gorilla

panda

deer

In the summer we go to the beach.
Clifford does the dog paddle.

umbrella

lighthouse

surfboard

towel

chair

bag

ball

dog

straw hat

picnic basket

sandwich

seagull

sunglasses

blanket

sun

seaplane

raft

ocean

lobster

sandpipers

seaweed

sand

horseshoe crab

pail

shovel

starfish

sand castle

Today is a special day!